Choices and Changes

Choices and Changes

Richard J. Smith

Perfection Learning
Logan, Iowa 51546

Cover and inside illustration: Art Ruiz

To my three daughters who shared these stories with my grandchildren and to my son and daughter-in-law who gave me their insights as teachers

CONTENTS

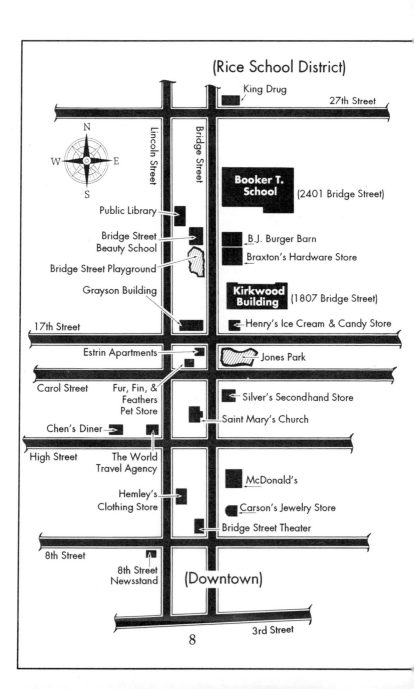

(Rice School District)

King Drug

27th Street

N
W   E
S

Lincoln Street

Bridge Street

Booker T. School (2401 Bridge Street)

Public Library

Bridge Street Beauty School

Bridge Street Playground

Grayson Building

B.J. Burger Barn

Braxton's Hardware Store

Kirkwood Building (1807 Bridge Street)

Henry's Ice Cream & Candy Store

17th Street

Estrin Apartments

Jones Park

Carol Street

Fur, Fin, & Feathers Pet Store

Silver's Secondhand Store

Saint Mary's Church

Chen's Diner

High Street

The World Travel Agency

McDonald's

Hemley's Clothing Store

Carson's Jewelry Store

Bridge Street Theater

8th Street

8th Street Newsstand

(Downtown)

3rd Street

8

INTRODUCTION

Bridge Street starts downtown and comes all the way to Booker T. Washington School. It goes even farther north. But Booker T. kids seldom go north of their school. North of Booker T. is Rice School District.

Most kids who go to Booker T. live in apartments. An apartment house with six floors stands at 1807 Bridge Street. It's called the Kirkwood Building. The kids who live there call themselves the Kirkwood Kids. Five of these kids are Keesha, Tracy, Martin, Pablo, and Li. They're good friends. All five are in the same grade at Booker T. Mrs. Anne Brown is their teacher. Mrs. Brown calls them the Kirkwood Five.

50, 100, 200, 220, 240, 260 . . . $287! Pablo's head is spinning. If he tries to return the money, 287 different people will claim it. Still, he can't keep it. The money isn't his. What can he do?

Finders Keepers?

The B. J. Burger Barn was on Bridge Street just three blocks from the Kirkwood Building. The Kirkwood Five didn't often have money to spend on fast food. But when they did, the Burger Barn got their business.

No one knew what the B. J. part stood for. The kids talked about their ideas on the way home from school one day.

"I think B. J. stands for 'Big and Juicy,' " said Tracy. "Just like the hamburgers!"

Keesha had other ideas. "Probably 'Big Gyp!' " she said. But then Li informed her that "gyp" was spelled with a "g," not a "j."

"So—who cares?" Keesha said. "They charge too much. And the burgers are too small!"

Still, the kids went to the Burger Barn every

chance they got. Like Saturday. Pablo had just finished selling papers. On Saturday and Sunday mornings, he often bought a stack of newspapers. Then he'd stand at the corner of Bridge and Carol Streets and sell the papers.

Of course, he couldn't make any profit on the papers. But some people would give him a tip. And this had been a good morning for tips.

Pablo was heading for the Burger Barn when Leon saw him. Leon lived in the Grayson Building. He was a year older, but he knew Pablo from baseball.

"Hey," Leon said as he ran to catch up with Pablo.

Pablo turned around. He smiled. "Hi, Leon. How about a burger? I'm buying."

"About time," Leon joked. "If you're buying, I'm eating." The two boys talked baseball as they walked into the Burger Barn together.

Inside Pablo ordered a shake. Leon ordered a burger and fries. Pablo got nervous. He didn't know if he'd have enough money for fries too. Still, he didn't want Leon to think he was cheap. "Want a shake too?" he asked. He was relieved when Leon shook his head.

"Just a small soda," Leon said. "You only having a shake?"

"Had a big breakfast," Pablo fibbed. He prayed he'd have enough money. Luckily, he did. They got their food and sat down at a booth.

"You hear how the Sox did last night?" Leon asked.

"Six to three. They moved up to third place."

"What about the Cubs?"

"Lost again. They'll be in the cellar before long," said Pablo.

When Pablo said *cellar,* he pointed his thumb at the floor. His eyes followed it. His thumb came up, but his eyes stayed on the floor.

"Hey, what are you looking at down there?" Leon asked.

Instead of answering, Pablo reached down. "It's money," he said quietly. "A lot of money!"

"How much?"

Pablo counted, "50, 100, 200, 220, 240, 260 . . . $287." He quickly stuffed it in his jacket pocket.

"Geez!" Leon exclaimed. "Who do you suppose lost it?"

"Whoever was in this booth before we came. Let's ask around. Find out who was sitting here."

"You're kidding, right? Keep it in your pocket, man. It's yours now."

"Maybe it was someone's paycheck or welfare

check. People around here don't have $287 to lose.''

Pablo asked the people sitting near the booth if they knew who had been sitting there. No one did.

''I'd better turn it in,'' he said to Leon.

''So who are you going to give it to?''

''I don't know.'' Pablo thought awhile. ''The boss, I guess.''

''The boss!'' Leon said. ''I know the boss of this place. He's a rat. Can't be trusted. Give him $287 today and he'll spend it tonight. He'll tell you he found whoever lost it and gave it back.'' Leon sounded like he knew what he was talking about.

''What should I do then?'' Pablo asked.

''Like I said before: keep it. You found it. You'll never find the real person who lost it. Tell the world you found $287, and 287 people will say they lost it.''

Pablo's thoughts went back and forth. *Leon makes sense. And there's a lot I could do with $287. I'd even give some to charity,* he thought.

But the money belongs to someone else. Someone else who probably really needs it!

''Let's get out of here,'' Pablo said. ''I can't think with all these people around.''

Quickly Pablo finished his shake. Leon gulped down his meal and grabbed his soda.

Once outside, Leon said he'd better go. "I'm meeting some guys at school. We're going to shoot some hoops. Thanks for the food," he said to Pablo. "And think about what I said. Keep the loot." Leon headed right.

Pablo turned left and walked toward Jones Park. It was always quiet there. Sometimes he went there when he needed to think something through. Like now.

Pablo sat down on a bench to think. A large black man sitting on a bench nearby caught his attention. The man was dressed in an expensive suit. A leather briefcase was open in his lap.

It was clear to Pablo that the man was searching for something. He looked through the papers in his case. Then he felt in all of his suit coat pockets. Finally he stood up and pushed his hands in his front and back pants pockets. He shook his head as if to say, "What's going on here?" The man looked up at the sound of a car on the gravel drive.

Pablo turned to see a limousine enter the park gate. It was a stretch limo with a TV antenna on the trunk. The car pulled up next to the man, and a chauffeur got out.

"Good afternoon, Mr. Jones," the chauffeur greeted him. "Are you ready to go, sir?"

"I'm ready, Bill. But would you take a look around this bench? I seem to have lost some money." They both searched the area for a minute or two.

"Well, that's the way it goes. I guess I'll have to be more careful. Let's go," the man said.

The chauffeur held the car door, and the man stepped into the limousine. The chauffeur walked around the car, got in the other side, and drove them away.

Pablo had watched it all. Then he noticed he wasn't alone. A police officer had been watching too.

"How would you like to have that parked in your garage?" the officer asked.

"Huh?" Pablo answered.

"The car," the officer said. "Isn't she a beauty?"

"Who was that?" Pablo asked. He was feeling a little shaky.

"That's Benjamin Jones. He owns half of the apartment buildings around here. People think this park is named after Mayor Henry Jones. But it isn't. It's named after Benjamin Jones. He gave the land to the city."

"Does he live around here?" Pablo asked. His voice felt weak.

"Not anymore. He grew up around here. Made a lot of money. But he comes back now and then. He likes to eat at the B. J. Burger Barn. He owns the place. Sometimes he eats there then walks over to this park. He owns the Bridge Street Movie Theater too."

Pablo's head was spinning. "Where does he live now?" His voice sounded far away.

"Across town. On Riverside Lane. He has a big estate there."

"I've got to go," Pablo said. He walked toward the park gate.

When he was back on Bridge Street, Pablo felt better. The familiar sounds and places cleared his head.

Two hundred eighty-seven dollars is peanuts to Benjamin Jones, thought Pablo. *He didn't even look for it for very long. He'll hardly miss it!*

But to Pablo, $287 meant a new baseball glove, movies, major league ball games, and lots of food for his friends and him at the B. J. Burger Barn.

Pablo walked down Bridge Street until he came to Saint Mary's Church. He stood for a minute. Then he turned and walked up the steep steps.

Padre Joseph always said, ''If you need advice, come to church. You'll find your best friend here.''

Pablo knelt in the back. Only a couple of other people were there. The sunlight coming through the windows made colored shadows. He took the money out of his pocket and counted it again. He thought about the $287.

I could give Padre Joseph $50 for the parish poor. Maybe even $100. Saint Mary's poor needs the money more than Benjamin Jones.

Pablo knelt awhile longer with his thoughts. Suddenly, he knew what he had to do. Pablo stood up and walked out of the church. He started running when he hit the sidewalk. In minutes he was at the Kirkwood Building. He flew up the steps and into his apartment.

''Grandma, do you have an envelope?''

''Is that you, Pablo?'' she answered from the bedroom.

''I need an envelope, Grandma,'' Pablo called to her.

''In the cupboard. Next to the Sunday dishes.''

Pablo found an envelope, took the money out of his pocket, and slipped it in. He sat down at the kitchen table. On the front of the envelope he wrote

Mr. Benjamin Jones
Riverside Lane

He added the name of the city and the state. He didn't know the zip code. But it wouldn't matter. The people at the post office would surely know who Mr. Benjamin Jones on Riverside Lane was.

"I'm going now, Grandma," he called. "I'll be back in about an hour."

And before Grandma could answer, Pablo was out the door. He put the envelope in his jacket pocket. He planned to buy a stamp at King Drug.

Pablo hurried up Bridge Street. But then in front of the Burger Barn he stopped short. The limousine! It was parked by the restaurant.

Pablo left the sidewalk and looked in the window. Benjamin Jones was sitting in the booth where Pablo had found the money.

Pablo knew he had to go in. He wasn't sure what he planned to do. But something drew him into the Barn.

Pablo walked through the door just as Mr. Jones motioned to a young man behind the counter. The young man slid into the booth with Mr. Jones. Pablo ordered a small soda and sat in

20

the booth behind Benjamin Jones. He listened.

"Sam," Mr. Jones was saying, "I lost some money earlier today. I think I might have lost it in here. Did anyone turn any money in to you?"

"No, sir," Sam answered. "And I've been here all day."

"Could the money have been turned in to someone else behind the counter?"

"I can check for you, sir. James has been here all day too," Sam said.

"I was almost home," Mr. Jones continued. "I was going to forget about the money. Then I thought I'd check with you, Sam."

Pablo could keep quiet no longer. "Mr. Jones, I found your money." Benjamin Jones turned around to look at Pablo.

"I was going to mail it to you," Pablo said. He reached for the envelope and handed it to Benjamin Jones. "See?"

Benjamin Jones read the address on the envelope. He looked at Pablo again. "Come here, son. Slide in next to Sam. Something tells me you have a story to tell."

The words spilled out. Pablo told everything. He ended by saying, "I really wanted to keep the money. But something wouldn't let me."

"What's your name?" Benjamin Jones asked.

"Pablo Gonzales. I live in the Kirkwood."

"I know about the Kirkwood. I grew up around here. And not that long ago either," said Mr. Jones. "So, what would you do with this much money?"

"Well, I thought about how I'd like to buy a new glove. I play for the Booker T. Hornets."

"Ah, yes. The Hornets. I used to play first base. Not bad, either. How much does a new glove cost these days, Pablo?" asked Mr. Jones.

"I saw a great one at Manson's for $40."

Benjamin Jones opened the envelope and handed Pablo some money. "That ought to do it," he said. "Anything else?"

Pablo thought again. "I thought about going to the movies."

"No problem." Mr. Jones reached into his suit coat pocket and pulled out a card. As he wrote on the card, he explained. "This is a pass for free movies for three months. Anything else?"

Pablo felt a little strange. But after all, Mr. Jones was asking. "Well, sir, I thought about tickets to a major league game."

"You a Sox fan?"

"Yes, sir!"

"Me too." Mr. Jones took out his wallet. "Here are three tickets to tomorrow's game.

Enjoy.'' Pablo's head was spinning again.

"Anything else?'' Benjamin Jones asked.

"There is one more thing I thought a lot about. I was going to give . . . '' Pablo paused. "Well, I was going to give Padre Joseph $50 for Saint Mary's poor people.''

Benjamin Jones reached into the envelope again. He handed Pablo the rest of the money. "Please see that Padre Joseph gets this.'' He put out his hand. "Always good to meet an honest man.'' Pablo shook Mr. Jones' hand and left.

Back on Bridge Street, Pablo's head was still spinning. As he headed down the street toward the Kirkwood, he saw Leon coming towards him.

"Hey, how's Mr. Rich Guy?'' asked Leon. "You keep that money?''

"Nah. I found the guy who lost it. I gave it back.''

"I don't know about you, Pablo! Want a burger? My treat.''

"No thanks, Leon. I've got to go see Padre Joseph. Say, want to watch the Sox play tomorrow?''

I would like to be your friend,
So to you this poem I send.

Keesha is thrilled! Lamar Bates wrote a poem especially for her. And he wants to be her friend. Wait until Pablo and Martin hear about this.

Keesha and Lamar Bates

The Estrin Apartments were two blocks south of the Kirkwood. Rent there was much higher than in the Kirkwood. Even higher than at the Grayson Building.

Keesha called the kids who lived there "Estrin rich kids." Or ERK for short. "Who cares? He's just an ERK," Keesha would say.

But Lamar Bates was a different story. He was an ERK, but Keesha thought he was great. He wrote poems that sang in her ears.

Martin and Pablo didn't share Keesha's feelings. They thought Lamar was weird, and they didn't mind telling Keesha so.

One day after school, Martin and Pablo overheard Keesha going on and on about Lamar.

24

"How can you like a weirdo like Bates?" Pablo asked. "He's a jerk."

"He can't even catch a baseball. And he could never hit one," Martin added.

"Any idiot can catch a baseball. And an even bigger idiot can hit one," Keesha shot back. "You guys are proof."

Neither Martin nor Pablo knew what to say. Before they could answer, Keesha had stomped away. When it came to arguing, Keesha always had the last word.

Pablo and Martin didn't like to lose an argument. And nobody called them idiots and got away with it! They decided to get even.

"Keesha thinks Lamar's so great. But he doesn't give two hoots about her," Martin said. "So he writes poems. Big deal!"

"I'd like to see Mr. Poetry throw a guy out at home plate from second base," added Pablo. "Lamar thinks he's so smart because Mrs. Brown likes his poetry. I think we need to teach Keesha and Lamar a lesson!"

"Great idea!" Martin said. "Let's get them both for acting so smart."

The boys thought and talked for a long time. Thinking of a way to get even with Keesha wasn't easy. It was even harder to think of a way to get her to see "Weirdo Bates" for what he was.

It was Pablo who finally came up with the plan. He explained.

"First, we'll make her think he likes her as much as she likes him," Pablo said.

"Okay. But how?" Martin asked. Pablo could always see the end of a plan better than Martin could.

"We'll send her a note asking her to walk home from school with him. We can sign his name. Ask her to meet him after school."

"But he won't show up," Martin said. The plan was still a little fuzzy to him.

"That's the idea. She'll think Lamar asked her to walk home with him and didn't bother to show up."

Martin thought for a while. "That'll get even with Keesha. But how will it hurt Lamar?"

"Think, Martin," Pablo answered. "What will Keesha do to someone who makes a fool of her?"

Now Martin was with the plan. "If I know Keesha, she'll let him have it. Both barrels."

"Right! You got it, Martin. They hurt each other, and we get even with both of them," said Pablo. Both boys smiled. They were pleased with their plan.

Pablo added the finishing touch. "We'll write

the note like a poem. That'll get Keesha. If 'Weirdo Bates' writes poetry to her, she'll melt.''

"Great idea," Martin agreed.

The plan was set. And the more they talked about it, the more they liked it. In fact, they were so proud of themselves, they had to brag to someone. This plan was too good to keep secret. Tracy walked up at the right moment.

Martin and Pablo looked at each other. The perfect person to tell. They both knew Tracy would never say a word. But she'd be dying to.

"Hey, Tracy. Come here," said Pablo. "Listen to this. But you have to promise not to tell." Then Pablo and Martin both started talking at once. Tracy listened.

What a rotten trick, thought Tracy. *Keesha will feel bad. Then she'll get even with Lamar. And Lamar won't even have done anything!* Tracy liked Pablo and Martin. But Keesha was her best friend.

"Why do you want to cause trouble?" Tracy asked the boys.

"Because Keesha always thinks she's so smart," Pablo answered.

"Someone needs to teach her a lesson," Martin added. "She's always bossing you around too."

"I can take care of myself, thank you." Tracy

was getting madder. "But why make trouble for Lamar?"

"Because he thinks he's better than we are. You can tell he thinks writing poems is better than playing baseball," Pablo answered.

"I think that's your problem. Lamar probably doesn't even think about baseball or you two guys. His poetry doesn't hurt anyone. Just leave him and Keesha alone," Tracy pleaded.

"Listen, Tracy," Pablo replied. "You promised not to tell."

"And I won't tell," Tracy assured them. "I never break a promise. But I don't have to stay here and listen to any more of your dumb plan. I think you're both just jealous."

"You better not spoil our joke," Martin called after her.

"Some joke!" Tracy shouted over her shoulder as she walked away. "You guys are the joke."

Tracy felt terrible knowing Keesha was going to be hurt, and she couldn't do anything about it. She felt sorry for Lamar too. But she'd promised not to tell.

On Thursday after school, Keesha ran up to Tracy. "Tracy, Tracy!" she said excitedly, but quietly. "Look at this." She handed Tracy a sheet of paper folded several times. "I found it in my

28

desk after recess.''

Tracy took the paper and unfolded it. She read the poem written on it.

> I would like to be your friend,
> So to you this poem I send.
> I think it would be cool,
> If you'd meet me Friday after school.
> Meet me at the playground gate.
> Please be there and don't be late.

Lamar Bates

''Not one of Lamar's best,'' Tracy said.

''It's not the words, Tracy. It's what they mean. Lamar wants to be my friend. He wants to walk home from school with me. Can you believe it?''

Tracy couldn't think of anything to say. She knew Martin and Pablo had written that poem. She also knew that Lamar wouldn't be there to meet Keesha.

Tracy could imagine Martin and Pablo watching and laughing as Keesha waited. She wanted to tell Keesha everything she knew. *Why can't Keesha see through all of this?* Tracy thought. *I guess people believe what they want to.*

Then another thought came to her. Tracy had an idea. Something that just might work.

"Let's get going," Tracy said as she handed the poem back to Keesha. They walked south on Bridge Street, Keesha chattering all the way.

"I just can't wait until tomorrow after school," Keesha said as she and Tracy parted in the hallway of the Kirkwood. "Isn't Lamar the greatest?"

Tracy nodded her head and opened the door to her apartment. "See you tomorrow." Tracy waved and went inside.

Once inside, Tracy sat down at the kitchen table and shouted hello to Aunt Bess.

Aunt Bess answered from the bedroom. Every afternoon at this time, she watched *Win the Jackpot*. Tracy could hear voices, music, and applause coming from the TV set.

Tracy knew what she had to do. She tore out a blank page from one of her notebooks. Then she started to write.

> I would like to be your friend,
> So to you this poem I send.

"Yuck!" she said to herself. Then she thought and wrote again.

I think it would be cool,
If you'd meet me Friday after school.

The last part was easy.

Meet me at the playground gate.
Please be there and don't be late.

 Keesha Johnson

Tracy sat back and read what she had written. She smiled. And no one could say she hadn't kept her promise.

"What's for supper, Aunt Bess?" Tracy called into the bedroom.

On the way to lunch the next day, Tracy was last in line. So it was easy to slip the folded paper into Lamar's desk. She put it right on top of everything else so he couldn't miss it.

Later at lunch, Tracy heard Keesha speak to Lamar as he walked past with his tray. "See you after school," Keesha said. Lamar had looked puzzled and said nothing. Tracy hoped that's all Keesha would say to Lamar.

Back in the room after lunch, Tracy watched Lamar. The first time Lamar opened his desk, she held her breath. Tracy saw him find the folded paper. He opened it, put it in his lap, and read it. He refolded the paper and slipped it back in his desk.

Other people in the class were thinking about Lamar too. Martin had been nervous all day. He was wondering if they had done the right thing. "What if Keesha finds out what we did?" Martin asked Pablo at recess.

"How can she?" Pablo replied. "Tracy's the only one who knows. And she's promised not to tell."

But Pablo wasn't feeling as good about their plan either. Back in the room, he nervously watched the clock on the wall as Friday afternoon ticked away.

At last the hands slipped down to 3:30 p.m. Mrs. Brown wished them all a good weekend and reminded them of their homework.

By 3:35 p.m., Keesha was at the playground gate. Martin and Pablo were there too, but out of sight. They stood behind the corner of the school. They could see Keesha, but she couldn't see them.

Tracy had the best view of all. She was sitting on a playground swing watching Martin, Pablo, and Keesha.

Martin and Pablo didn't enjoy watching Keesha as much as they thought they would.

They hadn't stood there too long before they decided to go.

Anyway, they knew what would happen. Keesha would get tired of waiting and leave.

"Let's go. We taught her a good lesson," Pablo said.

But just as Pablo and Martin started home, Lamar walked up to Keesha. Both boys ducked back behind the corner of the building.

"What's he doing here?" they said together.

"Looks like your plan didn't work," said a voice from the swings. The boys turned around to see Tracy coming towards them.

"Tracy!" Pablo said. "What are you doing here?"

"I wanted to watch you get even with Keesha and Lamar," Tracy answered. "Looks like your plan isn't working." The three of them watched Keesha and Lamar talking and walking down Bridge Street together.

"Did you have something to do with this?" Pablo asked Tracy.

"I promised not to tell. And I didn't," said Tracy.

"I think I'm almost glad it didn't work," Martin said.

"If you guys give him a chance, you might

even like Lamar. He's going to be Keesha's friend,'' Tracy said. ''And you shouldn't let what Keesha says bother you. You know she talks without thinking. She doesn't mean a lot of what she says.''

''I know. It's just that she makes me so mad sometimes,'' said Pablo.

''I guess Keesha's okay. She's just a big talker,'' said Martin. ''Lamar's probably okay too. Maybe he'd like to play baseball if we'd teach him how.''

''And maybe he could teach you two to write better poems. You could use some lessons!''

They laughed and walked down Bridge Street behind Keesha and Lamar Bates.

Li can't believe it! Brad Weeks has invited her to a party at his house Friday night. Brad is older than Li and very popular. And Li is the only one in Mrs. Brown's class who's been invited. Li feels very special. There's just one small problem. Her parents told her she can't go.

Brad's Party

Li Chen was friends with everyone. It was easy to like her. So it was not surprising that she got asked to a lot of parties.

Mrs. Brown thought going to parties was an important part of growing up. "Helps to develop the social graces," was what she said to parents at Parents' Night at School.

"But for my students, daytime parties only," she'd add. "The kids in my class are too young to go to parties at night."

Some parents thought Mrs. Brown was too old-fashioned. But most agreed with her. Parents even quoted Mrs. Brown when they refused to let their children go to parties at night.

Li's parents agreed with Mrs. Brown. They

were proud of Li and trusted her. But they were also very careful.

Whenever Li was asked to a party, there were certain things her parents needed to know. First, they wanted to talk to the parents of the person having the party. "We must be sure an adult will be there," they told Li.

They also had to know when the party would start and end. And if her parents didn't know the person giving the party, they would have to meet her friend.

"Maybe I should just stay home," Li pouted one time. For her remark, her parents made her do just that!

"A girl who cannot control her tongue is not old enough to go to parties," her father said. And that was that. Her parents were very strict.

Grandfather, on the other hand, was a little more patient with Li. He would listen to Li's opinion when she didn't agree. Oh sure, he didn't let her do whatever she wanted. But at least he listened to her. Once in a while, he even reminded Li's parents that they had been young once themselves. Li was glad Grandfather lived with them.

So when Brad Weeks invited Li to his Friday-night party, she went to Grandfather. Brad lived in the Estrin Apartments. Li knew him from school even though he was a grade ahead of her.

"He's the most popular boy in school," Li gushed. "And I'm the only one in Mrs. Brown's class who's invited."

Li continued. She talked fast. She had to make Grandfather understand. "Please help me, Grandfather. Mother and Father will listen to you. Tell them I'm more grown-up than they think. They're just being old-fashioned. I'm old enough to go to a party on Friday night. Please tell them. They'll listen to you."

Grandfather was silent for a long time. Li could hardly stand the silence.

At last, Grandfather spoke. "Li, you are wise for your years. But your years do not number many. And only years can bring us wisdom.

"Today you feel grown-up enough to go to that boy's party. But when you are your parents' age, you'll know that you were not. You cannot know what they know because you do not have their years. They cannot know what I know for the same reason," added Grandfather.

"Trust us. Both your parents and I know this party will not bring you happiness. Everything in good time, my granddaughter."

Li knew her grandfather well. He had spoken his mind. He wouldn't change it.

He's even more old-fashioned than Mother and Father, Li thought. *Sure, I'm younger. But there are some things they don't understand because they're so much older. I'm going to that party. I'll find a way.*

Next morning, Li was still determined to carry out her plan. When she saw Brad in the hall at school, she called out, "See you Friday night. What time should I be there?"

"Don't come before 9:00," Brad answered. "My parents won't be gone before then."

"Oh, your parents won't be home?" Li tried not to sound surprised.

"You're kidding, right?" Brad said with a smile. He gave Li's shoulder a small shove. "I'm glad you're coming. See you later." Brad ran to catch up with some friends.

Li felt ashamed and guilty. She didn't have her parents' permission. And now she knew there would be no adults at the party. Her parents would never approve.

Li knew she had two choices. She could tell Brad that she couldn't come. Or she could go to the party as she told Brad she would. Asking her parents wasn't one of her choices.

Well, she'd already made up her mind. "I'm

going to that party," she said to herself. But that meant she had some serious planning to do. She had to get out of the apartment without Grandfather seeing her. Then she had to think of a way to sneak back in. *I'll think of a plan by Friday,* she thought.

On Wednesday, Li should have felt excited, but she didn't. When she got a 60 percent on a spelling test, Mrs. Brown asked her if she was sick. Li said she felt fine, but it wasn't true. At night, she was having bad dreams. And she was nervous all day.

Li felt guilty every time she looked at her parents or Grandfather. She couldn't even talk to her friends about the party. She was afraid to. The news could get back to her parents.

Li's friends noticed the change. Thursday morning, Tracy asked her why she was so quiet. Keesha said she was acting weird.

"Hey, Li, are you playing Monopoly at Keesha's Friday night?" asked Tracy. Li started to shake her head, but she stopped. A plan began forming in her mind.

"Monopoly? Friday night? At Keesha's apartment?" Li paused after each question. "Gee. I'd like to, but I can't."

Li thought fast. "I promised my parents I'd

help out at the restaurant. They're open until 10:00 Friday nights.''

That's it! She was thinking fast now. ''So I won't be home Friday night.'' She had told another lie. This time to her best friends.

Li was beginning to wonder if Brad's party was worth it. But she'd made up her mind. She was going to the party and that was that.

Friday morning, Li rehearsed her plan in her mind. *Tell Grandfather I'm playing Monopoly and sleeping over at Keesha's. Leave our apartment at 7 p.m. Hang around the Kirkwood but stay out of sight until 9:00. Walk slowly two blocks south to the Estrin Apartments. Arrive at the party about 9:10.*

This will work, Li thought. *When the party's over, walk home with some other kids. Knock on our door, which will be locked. Tell whoever comes to the door that I had a fight with Keesha and decided to come home. Neat!*

Li was pleased with her plan. She went over it several more times to be sure she hadn't missed anything. *It'll work,* she thought. *Then why do I feel so scared?* she wondered. *And why don't I feel happy?*

Supper for Grandfather, Li, and her little brother Sam was at 6:00 on Friday nights. Li's parents ate supper at their restaurant.

Li didn't worry about homework on Friday nights. After supper, she'd do the dishes while Grandfather put Sam to bed. Then she and Grandfather would settle in to watch *Mystery Theater*.

Around 10:00, Li would go to bed. Usually, Grandfather fell asleep in front of the TV. He would get up to go to bed around 11:00 when Li's parents got home. It was the same every Friday night.

But not this Friday night. Li was finishing the dishes when Grandfather came into the living room. "Sam is sound asleep," he said. "We will have quiet for *Mystery Theater*."

"Grandfather, have you forgotten? I am playing at Keesha's tonight." Li paused, and her voice grew weak. "And sleeping over."

Grandfather looked into her eyes. "Ah, yes. I remember. But I thought perhaps your plans had changed."

Li felt miserable. She didn't like what she was doing. And she disliked herself for doing it. But she tried to sound cheerful. "Oh, Grandfather. We always watch *Mystery Theater*. One Friday night won't hurt."

"I see," Grandfather said. "Then I must watch it alone." He looked sad.

Li couldn't bear to be near her grandfather a minute longer. She wanted to tell him it was all a lie. That she was really going to Brad's party. That she had lied about staying at Keesha's. That she wasn't being honest with her friends and her family.

"I've got to go now," Li blurted out. "Keesha and Tracy are waiting for me." She ran out of the apartment and down the stairs.

When Li reached the front door of the Kirkwood, she paused. The night air was cool. And Li didn't have her coat. *I couldn't take my coat and say I was going to Keesha's,* she thought. But she wished she had it.

Li looked at her watch. It was barely 7:00. Two hours to kill. She began to walk north on Bridge Street.

The street was busy and well lit. Some people were headed for home while others were shopping. A few were just enjoying an evening walk. The many people on the street cheered Li a little.

She began to relax and think of the fun she would soon be having at Brad's party. Best of all, she was the only one in her class Brad had invited.

Li took her time looking in all of the store windows. Then she sat on a bench at a bus stop for a while. She left quickly when she saw the bus coming.

When Li passed King Drug, she glanced at the clock on the wall. 8:15. Another hour to kill.

Li thought of home. *Mystery Theater* would be half over. Keesha and Tracy would still be playing Monopoly—unless Keesha had gotten bored and turned on the TV. She wondered how the rest of Mrs. Brown's students were spending this Friday night.

If she didn't walk too fast, she could retrace her steps and not reach the Estrin Apartments before 9:00. Bridge Street would be bright and busy until then.

The next hour passed more quickly. At 9:10, Li walked up the front steps of the Estrin Apartments. Right on schedule. Her plan was working.

Li was nervous and excited as she pushed the doorbell at Brad's apartment door. Li heard music and loud talking and laughing inside. *At least I'm not the first to arrive,* she thought.

A girl answered the door. Li recognized her as someone in Brad's class. "Hi," she said. "Who are you?"

"I'm Li Chen," Li answered.

The girl turned her back to Li and called into

the apartment. "Brad, your little friend is here."

Brad came to the door. "Oh, hi, Li. I forgot you were coming. Come on in and join the fun."

Li stepped into the room. The music was very loud. Three kids were dancing in the middle of the living room. The furniture had been pushed back against the walls. Brad left Li and joined in the dancing.

Li noticed other kids in the kitchen. And the doorbell kept announcing more and more arrivals.

Everyone seemed to know everyone else. Li had seen most of them at school. But no one seemed to know who she was. Then one boy saw Li standing by herself and shouted, "Hey, Brad. Why don't you introduce your little friend?"

"Later," Brad called. "Get yourself a soda from the fridge, Li."

Li walked into the kitchen. She felt alone, embarrassed, and a little afraid. The kids in the kitchen were standing in front of the refrigerator. No one seemed to notice or move aside for her. She took a warm soda from the counter and opened it.

She walked back into the living room just as one of the dancers tripped and knocked over a lamp. "Don't worry about it," Brad yelled. "We had too much light in here anyway."

Then Brad saw Li. "Hey, Li," he called to her. "Come on and dance."

Li didn't know how to dance, so she shook her head. But Brad grabbed her hand and pulled her into the middle of the living room. The soda she was carrying splashed onto her dress.

Soon everyone knew that Li couldn't dance. But Brad kept her in the middle of the floor anyway. All the other kids formed a circle around them. They were laughing and clapping.

Someone shouted, "The next dance is mine, kid." Everybody laughed. Li's face had never felt so hot. Nor had her heart ever felt so heavy. Then the music stopped.

Everyone looked at the boy who had been playing the music. Li looked too. The boy had moved away from the sound system. An old man stood next to him.

"I'm sorry to interrupt your party," the old man said. "But I'm afraid I must ask my granddaughter to leave early. You see, we have a family problem, and she is needed at home."

The circle around Li opened to make a path for her. She walked slowly to Grandfather Chen.

"Now," the old man said to the group, "please go on with your party." He took Li's hand and led her out of the apartment, out of the building, and up Bridge Street.

The two walked in silence. When they reached the front steps, Li asked, "How did you know, Grandfather?"

"I listened to your words, but your eyes told me a different story," said Grandfather.

"How did you find the party?" asked Li.

"It's not hard to find a noisy party in the Estrin Apartments."

Li remembered Sam. "Who's with Sam?"

"Mrs. Hudson is with him. It is nice to have a neighbor who is always home," added Grandfather.

"And the family problem you spoke of at the party?"

"You, my granddaughter. You are the family problem tonight."

"What time is it?"

"Barely 10:00. Your mother and father are not yet home."

"And will you tell them?"

"Some things are best left untold."

"You are wonderful, Grandfather," said Li.

"Perhaps. And perhaps I am just an old man who sees himself in his granddaughter. Come upstairs now. It is time for Mrs. Hudson to go home and for you to go to bed."

"Mr. Grant is studying to be a teacher," Mrs. Brown told the class in January. "He'll be with us for the rest of the school year." A student teacher— what a great opportunity to act up. And with Mr. Grant, it's so easy!

A New Year, A New Teacher

Pablo was daydreaming. His math book was open in front of him, but Pablo wasn't looking at it. Instead, he stared out the classroom window, thinking about summer.

It was the first week in June. Pablo and the other students at Booker T. were getting restless. The trees and flowers in Jones Park told them that summer vacation was just around the corner.

Pablo put his chin in his hand. He leaned into the sunny part of his desk. It was hard to keep his mind on math.

"Your work finished, Pablo?" Mr. Grant's voice cut through Pablo's dreams. Pablo sat up and looked at his math book. Mr. Grant cleared

his throat and headed on down the aisle.

Hubert Grant was Mrs. Brown's student teacher. Every year Mrs. Brown had a student from City College work with her.

"Mr. Grant is studying to be a teacher," Mrs. Brown had told the class in January. "He'll be with us for the rest of the school year."

The Kirkwood Five had had student teachers before. Some were good teachers, and the kids respected them. But some, like Mr. Grant, let the kids get away with a lot. Too much!

The kids complained that Mr. Grant was boring too. They missed Mrs. Brown's teaching.

Mrs. Brown would say, "Boys and girls, Mr. Grant is a teacher in this room. I expect you to behave for him the way you do for me."

So when Mrs. Brown was around, the kids behaved. But when she wasn't around . . .

By next fall, Mr. Grant would have a class of his own. Mrs. Brown's class felt sorry for the kids who were going to get him as their teacher. "They'll be bored to death," Keesha predicted.

But Mrs. Brown's class put up with Mr. Grant. After all, they had no choice.

And at last, the final days of school came and went. Everyone said good-bye. Mrs. Brown told them what a good class they had been. She told them to be just as good with Mr. Wilson next year.

In turn, several kids promised to stop in to see her next year. "You're the best teacher I've ever had," many of them told her. Some even fibbed and told Mr. Grant he had been a good teacher.

Then school was out. Hip, Hip, Hooray! Three months with nothing to do but

Sleep late

Go on picnics

Stay up late

Go swimming

Play basketball

Play baseball

Watch TV

Ride skateboards

Read books

Hang out

Have water fights

Eat ice cream

****

Those three months passed very quickly. Pablo, Keesha, Martin, Li, and Tracy sat on the front steps of the Kirkwood Building. It was a warm August night with lots of stars.

"I can't believe it," Li thought aloud. "Summer's over."

"Seems like it just started."

"It was too short."

"It was fun."

"I can't go back to school. Not yet."

"We have to go back!"

Pablo summed it up. "We're all going back to good old Booker T." He paused. "Tomorrow."

The next morning, all five kids met in front of the Kirkwood. The routine they knew so well was starting again. Walk down Bridge Street. Into the school. Down the hall. But this year they would not turn into Mrs. Brown's room.

Mrs. Brown had been a good teacher. The Kirkwood Five knew they would miss her. But they looked forward to a year with Mr. Wilson.

Mr. Wilson was a popular teacher. He was known as strict but fair. He had a good sense of humor. Every morning he started class with a joke.

Former students talked about the neat poems and stories Mr. Wilson read to the class. Sometimes, they said, he'd let his class sit back and listen to music together. Mr. Wilson called those times a "stress rest."

The five passed Mrs. Brown's door. They walked into Mr. Wilson's class together. "He's writing something on the board," Tracy whispered to Keesha. His back was to the classroom as his right hand printed ''WELCOME BACK'' on the chalkboard.

''Good morning, Mr. . . . '' The man at the chalkboard turned before Keesha could finish. ''Grant?''

''Good morning, Keesha,'' Mr. Hubert Grant answered. ''Welcome back. Please take your seats so we can begin.''

Once the class was seated, Mr. Grant spoke. ''Mr. Wilson transferred to Rice School. I was lucky enough to be asked to fill his position.''

No one knew what to say. They were stunned. Even Troy didn't get off his usual morning wisecracks.

Throughout the room, the students were all thinking the same thing. *Mr. Grant! For a whole year!*

Maybe he'll be better this year, Tracy thought.

Sadly, Tracy was wrong. Mr. Grant had not improved over the summer. The first week passed slowly.

The kids expected Mr. Grant to be boring, and he was. It didn't matter what he did. The class knew he wouldn't make them pay attention, so they didn't.

Troy just made things worse. He was always

starting trouble. He would do or say things to interrupt. Other students would laugh or even imitate him. No one listened to Mr. Grant.

Soon others kids began to cause trouble too. Even students who had never caused problems. Like Marc and Li.

One morning as the class worked on math, Marc left his seat and went to the pencil sharpener. Mr. Grant was at the front of the room working with a small group.

Suddenly Marc called out, ''Must be lunchtime.'' The class and Mr. Grant looked up. Marc repeated, ''Must be lunchtime.'' Then he added, ''This sharpener is so hungry, it's eating my pencil.''

It wasn't a very good joke, but the class laughed loudly. Troy held his sides and rolled on the floor. As usual, Mr. Grant had a hard time settling the class down.

Even Li stopped worrying about getting her work finished. Instead she wasted time by passing notes. In Mrs. Brown's class, the kids never passed notes. But that was last year.

Once Mr. Grant saw Li and Keesha passing notes back and forth. The girls had been writing about how boring he was. When he took the note from them and read it to himself, he looked embarrassed. Everyone laughed except Li and Keesha.

Poor Mr. Grant. It seemed he was getting worse rather than better.

The morning after the note passing, Mr. Grant began class with a joke. It wasn't a great joke, but if Mr. Wilson or Mrs. Brown had told it, the class would have laughed. For Mr. Grant, they groaned.

Then Troy jumped up and did a duck imitation. Only instead of quacking, he said, "Yuck, yuck, yuck," over and over again. Mr. Grant said, "Well, let's get started checking your math papers. I guess I don't tell jokes that well."

On the way home from school that afternoon, the Kirkwood Five talked about their teacher. Tracy started the conversation.

"I know he's boring and has trouble with the kids. But I'm learning a lot of math," Tracy added.

"I thought today's social studies lesson was fun," Pablo added.

"He's okay, I guess. But he's not Mrs. Brown," Martin said. And the subject was closed.

The next morning, Mrs. Smith, the school principal, came in to watch Mr. Grant teach. The kids saw this as a great chance to act up.

Mr. Grant asked an easy question and called

on Martin. "Gee, Mr. Grant, I don't think you told us about that." The class snickered.

For a lot of his questions, the kids just didn't raise their hands. Or they said they didn't know. Mr. Grant looked nervous. It was clear he didn't know what to do. Mrs. Smith finally left.

That afternoon during recess, Troy and two other kids made plans for "the greatest joke ever." It was Troy's idea. He wanted to smuggle a dog into the classroom.

"Imagine old Grant dancing around the room trying to catch a dog," Troy told the others. His plan took form.

There were always stray dogs and cats hanging around in the alley behind the school at lunchtime. They waited for the cooks to throw them some scraps. Troy knew he could sneak one of the strays into the classroom after lunch.

The next day, their plan unfolded. After lunch, Troy and Chris sneaked around the building. Troy grabbed a small, white dog and wrapped it in his jacket. Then he got in line to go back into the classroom. Other kids crowded around him. The playground teacher couldn't see that he was carrying a dog.

Pablo crowded up next to Troy. "He sounds mad," Pablo whispered. The dog was growling and trying to escape from Troy's arms. But Troy held him tightly.

The class walked inside and crowded through the door of the classroom. They shut the door behind them. Mr. Grant hadn't returned from the teachers' room yet.

Once the door was closed, Troy released the dog. He was angry and scared. When Tracy tried to pet him, he growled and showed his teeth.

The students all called to him at the same time.

"Here, boy."

"Come on, boy. Come to Keesha."

"Don't be scared, doggie."

The dog barked and whirled from one to another. Just as Troy reached down to pick up the dog, the door opened. Mr. Grant entered the room.

"What's going on here?" he shouted over the noise and confusion. His voice startled everybody, including the dog. With one quick snap, the dog had Troy's arm in his mouth. He growled through clenched teeth and started shaking Troy's arm.

Troy yelled, "Help me! Hey! Somebody help me! He's biting my arm!"

Some kids started screaming. A few ran to the other side of the room. Others just stood and watched.

In a second, Mr. Grant was at Troy's side. Mr. Grant grabbed the dog. His strong hands opened the dog's mouth and released Troy. Troy jumped back and rubbed his arm. His only injury was a torn sweatshirt.

The dog trembled in Mr. Grant's arms. Mr. Grant talked softly to him. "Easy, fella. Take it easy. It's all right now. Slow down, fella."

Soon the dog was quiet. Then Mr. Grant calmly said to the class, "Take your seats. I want you to read your library books while I take this dog back outside. And I don't want any talking while I'm gone."

When Mr. Grant returned, the kids were reading quietly. No one had talked, and no notes had been passed. The rest of the day went smoothly.

No one said much about the dog after that day. Not even Troy. But things changed.

A month passed, and Mr. Grant's students settled into school. They now enjoyed Mr. Grant's new ideas. And he enjoyed his students.

The kids never thought of Mr. Grant as "boring" again. They even bragged about him to their friends in other classes. "Mr. Grant's the best teacher," they were heard to say.

One afternoon Martin raised his hand. "What

is it, Martin?'' Mr. Grant asked.

"Would you ask Mrs. Smith to come in and watch you teach again? I think we're all a lot smarter now.''

The whole class cheered.

The Kids Help Out
(A Teledrama)

(The following teledrama is written in three parts. If you wish, you may write a short commercial to introduce each part. The three places where the commercials can be read are marked Voice 1, Voice 2, and Voice 3. The other characters in the teledrama are the announcer, Keesha, Tracy, Martin, Pablo, Li, Mr. Chen, Maria Martinez, and the circus ringmaster.)

Announcer:

Get ready for another SATURDAY
MORNING WITH THE KIRKWOOD KIDS
brought to you by (*mention sponsor*).
Today's feature is "The Kids Help Out."
Before we begin, here's a word from our
sponsor.

Voice 1:

[*Read your commercial.*]

Announcer:

And now for today's adventure: "The Kids Help Out." As our story begins, Keesha, Tracy, Martin, and Pablo are sitting on the front steps of the Kirkwood Building. It is 11:00 on a Saturday morning. Li is helping at her parents' restaurant.

Keesha:

You guys have any money?

Tracy:

I don't.

Martin:

Me either.

Pablo:

Neither do I. I didn't sell many newspapers this morning. And no tips.

Keesha:

Too bad. I'd sure like a B. J. Burger Barn shake.

Tracy:
And some fries.

Martin:
And a burger or two—or three or four
or . . .

Pablo:
Quiet!

(*They quickly stop talking.*)

Do you hear what I hear?

Martin:
What?

Pablo:
My stomach's growling.

Keesha:
Who cares?

Tracy:
Hey, guys. Let's go visit Li. Maybe she
could spare an egg roll or two.

(The four kids head down Bridge Street toward Chen's Diner. They go around to the kitchen door at the back of the restaurant. When Pablo knocks, Li opens the door.)

Li:

Boy, am I glad to see you guys! I need your help.

Tracy:

What do you mean? Is something wrong?

Li:

Nothing's wrong. It's just that there are so many people ordering lunch, we can't keep up.

Pablo:

How can we help?

Li:

My dad said if you guys stopped by, you could help me wait on tables.

Martin:

Do we get paid?

Li:

Two dollars an hour and all your tips.

Pablo:

Wow! Tips at last!

Keesha:

Let's get started. I might get that shake after all.

Tracy:

And fries.

Martin:

And burgers, burgers, burgers.

Announcer:

Stay tuned. The Kirkwood Kids will be right back. But first, a word from our sponsor.

Voice 2:

[*Read your commercial.*]

Announcer:

And now back to SATURDAY MORNING WITH THE KIRKWOOD KIDS. Today's adventure is called ''The Kids Help Out.'' As we return, Mr. Chen is giving the four kids white aprons.

Tracy:

How can we help, Mr. Chen?

Mr. Chen:

Look.

(*The kids look at a crowded dining room.*)

Keesha:

Holy smokestacks. Who are they?

Pablo:

Hey! That guy's got a monkey on a leash.

Martin:

Is that a clown?

Tracy:

Look at that man in a red suit and a tall black hat!

Mr. Chen:

That's the ringmaster. There's a circus in town. Some of the performers are here for lunch. Now hurry. Li will tell you what to do.

Li:

When people sit at one of your tables, take their order. The menu is on the wall. Write what they order on one of these checks. Give the check to Mom or Dad in the kitchen. They'll put the prices on the check, add it up, and give the food to you. You give the food and the check to the customer. They pay Dad at the counter when they leave. (*She points out which tables they each should cover.*)

Martin:

Sounds easy. Let's go.

Pablo:

Let's see who gets the most tips. We're out of here!

(*He heads out of the kitchen and into the dining area. The others are not far behind him.*)

Keesha:

Wow! Your dad wasn't kidding. But the circus isn't in town. It's in Chen's Diner! Come on, guys. Let's feed them.

Announcer:

Don't go away. We'll be back in a few minutes with the exciting finish to ''The Kids Help Out.'' But first, another word from our sponsor.

Voice 3:

[*Read your commercial.*]

Announcer:

And now back to "The Kids Help Out."
The lunch hour is over. The last customer
is paying his bill at the counter. He and
Mr. Chen are visiting. The kids are sitting
at a table, resting.

Keesha:

Boy, that's hard work, Li.

Pablo:

How did you guys do with tips?

Keesha:

Well. (*She pauses.*) Everybody gave me a
tip.

Tracy:

Me too.

Martin:

Me too.

Li:

Me too.

Pablo:

Everybody gave me a tip too, only . . .

Keesha:

Only what?

Pablo:

Only they all gave me a free pass to the circus. I've got seven free passes.

Keesha:

I've got six.

Tracy:

I've got eight.

Martin:

I've got five.

Li:

I've got ten.

Keesha:

Thirty-six free passes. What are we going to do with thirty-six passes?

Pablo:

These aren't the tips I had in mind, but I know how we can make a lot of money with these passes.

Martin:

How?

Pablo:

We can sell them to people on the way to the circus. Half price. They'll sell faster than peanuts at a Sox game.

Keesha, Tracy, and Li:

(*Together.*) Great idea!

(The front door opens, and a well-dressed woman walks in. She walks up to cash register. The kids listen as she talks to Mr. Chen.)

Woman:

Excuse me? Are you Mr. Chen?

Mr. Chen:

(*He stops talking to the man.*) Yes, ma'am. I'm the owner.

Woman:

My name is Maria Martinez. (*She shakes hands with Mr. Chen.*) I work as a volunteer for the Bridge Street Shelter. I'm collecting donations to take children from the shelter to see the circus. Would you care to sponsor some children?

(*Before Mr. Chen has a chance to speak, the kids ask one another a question with their eyes. They all nod their heads.*)

Li:

(*Jumps up.*) Dad, we can help!

Tracy:

We have thirty-six free passes.

Keesha:

Will thirty-six passes help?

Woman:

That would be great!

(*The five kids hand their passes to Ms. Martinez.*)

Tracy:

How many more tickets do you need for the homeless children?

Woman:

Only a few more. I was hoping to collect enough money for fifty tickets.

Man:

I think I might be able to help. I'm the circus ringmaster. Here are another fourteen passes for the children in the shelter. (*He hands the passes to Ms. Martinez. Then he turns to the Kirkwood Five.*)

I like what you guys did. But now you need more passes. (*He hands another free pass to each of them.*)

Mr. Chen:

(*Reaches into the cash register.*) And here's the money I owe you for helping out.

Pablo:

Wow! This is great!

Man:

One more thing. I could use some kids to ride in the circus wagon for the parade down Bridge Street this afternoon. How about it? Would you guys have the time?

All:

(*Taking off their aprons and caps.*) Are you kidding? Show us the way!